AR Ø

W9-BVK-372

Tadpoles

The Sad Princess

DISCARD

Crabtree Publishing Company
www.crabtreebooks.com
1-800-387-7650

PMB 16A, 350 Fifth Ave.
Suite 3308,
New York, NY

616 Welland Ave.
St. Catharines, ON
L2M 5V6

Published by Crabtree Publishing in 2010

Series Editor: Jackie Hamley
Editor: Reagan Miller
Series Advisor: Dr. Hilary Minns
Series Designer: Peter Scoulding
Editorial Director: Kathy Middleton

Text © Lynne Benton 2007
Illustration © Andy Catling 2007

The rights of the author and the illustrator
of this Work have been asserted.

All rights reserved. No part
of this publication may be
reproduced, stored in a retrieval
system, or transmitted in any
form or by any means, electronic,
mechanical, photocopy, recording
or otherwise, without the prior
written permission of the copy-
right owner.

First published in 2007
by Franklin Watts
(A division of Hachette
Children's Books)

**Library and Archives Canada
Cataloguing in Publication**

Benton, Lynne
 The sad princess / Lynne Benton ; illustrated by
Andy Catling.

(Tadpoles)
ISBN 978-0-7787-3872-5 (bound).--
ISBN 978-0-7787-3903-6 (pbk.)

     1. Readers (Primary). 2. Readers--Princesses.
3. Readers--Sadness. I. Catling, Andy II. Title.
III. Series: Tadpoles (St. Catharines, Ont.)

PE1117.T33 2009h   428.6   C2009-903990-7

**Library of Congress
Cataloging-in-Publication Data**

Benton, Lynne.
 The sad princess / by Lynne Benton ; illustrated
by Andy Catling.
     p. cm. -- (Tadpoles)
 Summary: The princess is so sad that no one can
cheer her up, until two naughty monkeys come to
the palace.
 ISBN 978-0-7787-3903-6 (pbk.) -- ISBN
978-0-7787-3872-5 (reinforced library binding)
 [1. Princesses--Fiction. 2. Monkeys--Fiction.
3. Sadness--Fiction.] I. Catling, Andy, ill. II. Title.
III. Series.

PZ7.B44755Sad 2010
[E]--dc22
                                              2009025300

The Sad Princess

by Lynne Benton

Illustrated by Andy Catling

Crabtree Publishing Company

www.crabtreebooks.com

Lynne Benton

"If you are feeling sad, like the Princess, then I hope this book will make you laugh!"

Andy Catling

"Being sad makes me mad which makes me sadder and so I get madder!"

The Princess was sad.

"A bag of gold to anyone who can make her laugh!" said the King.

A clown came.

But the Princess did
not laugh.

A magician came.

Still the Princess did
not laugh.

14

A boy came with
two monkeys.

They were very naughty.

The King was not very happy.

But the Princess
laughed and laughed.

21

"Can I keep them?"
asked the Princess.

"Yes," said the boy.
"Oh no!" said the King.

Notes for adults

TADPOLES are structured to provide support for early readers. The stories may also be used by adults for sharing with young children.

Starting to read alone can be daunting. **TADPOLES** help by providing visual support and repeating high frequency words and phrases. These books will both develop confidence and encourage reading and rereading for pleasure.

If you are reading this book with a child, here are a few suggestions:

1. Make reading fun! Choose a time to read when you and the child are relaxed and have time to share the story.
2. Talk about the story before you start reading. Look at the cover and the blurb. What might the story be about? Why might the child like it?
3. Encourage the child to reread the story, and to retell the story in their own words, using the illustrations to remind them what has happened.
4. Discuss the story and see if the child can relate it to their own experiences, or perhaps compare it to another story they know.
5. Give praise! Children learn best in a positive environment.

If you enjoyed this book, why not try another TADPOLES story?